MACHO NACHO & THE COWBOY BATTLE

Book 1 – Tuff, Sadie & The Wild West
Book 2 – General Muster & No-Trees Town
Book 3 – Grizzly Bears & Beaver Pelts
Book 4 – Macho Nacho & The Cowboy Battle
Book 5 – The Parrot Gang & Wild West Ghosts

Coming soon:
Book 6 – Billy the Kid & Crooked Jim
Book 7 – Judge Roy Bean & Wild Thing

MACHO NACHO

& THE COWBOY BATTLE

Hideout Kids Book 4

by

Mike Gleason

Illustrated by Victoria Taylor

FARM STREET PUBLISHING

First published 2017 by Farm Street Publishing
www.hideoutkidsbooks.com

Paperback ISBN 978-1-912207-09-1
Hardback ISBN 978-1-912207-10-7
eBook ISBN 978-1-912207-11-4

A CIP catalogue record for this book is available from
the British Library.

Design and typesetting by Head & Heart

To Michelle and Luke,
who inspired me to write these stories
of the Wild West.

TUFF

SADIE

CONTENTS

Dear Reader,

Did you ever wonder where the words "cowboy" and "cowgirl" come from? In *Macho Nacho & The Cowboy Battle*, the fourth in the series of Hideout Kids books, you'll find the answer.

The Wild West featured Trail Drives, where cows were gathered together into herds. The herds were walked, or "driven", from ranches around the West along trails to railroad towns such as Wichita, Kansas. From there, the cattle were loaded on to trains and carried to the large cities of the eastern United States like Chicago and New York City. The best steakhouses in those cities featured "Texas Longhorn Cattle".

The tough, brave boys and girls who "drove" the valuable cattle became known as cowboys and cowgirls.

Unfortunately outlaws began to steal cattle from the Trail Drives. The outlaws were called "rustlers" because they stole, or "rustled" cattle from the herds. It was hard to identify cattle which had been stolen so ranchers began to "brand" their cattle. Blacksmiths in the towns made iron rods with a design on the end. Each ranch had its own unique brand. The branding irons were heated up in a hot fire then the brand was placed on the tough hide of the cattle, where it would burn the unique design into the hide. Soon buyers of the cattle would only pay for them if they were branded. That way they knew they were not buying "stolen goods".

If you want to curl up with a good story, start curling and turn the page.

Mike Gleason

TUFF AND SADIE'S JOURNEY TO HELP CHARLIE 'SIR' RINGO

INDIAN TERRITORY

Fort Worth

AUSTIN

La Grange

Dime Box

Colorado River

TEXAS

GULF OF MEXICO

Rio Grande River

MACHO NACHO & THE COWBOY BATTLE

CHAPTER ONE

HONEYBEES

It was noon on a hot June day in the Wild West Texas town of Muleshoe.

Sheriff Tuff Brunson walked down Muleshoe's dusty Main Street. He felt lazy. Thousands of cicadas buzzed in the mesquite trees around the town. *What should I have for lunch today?* he wondered as he neared the Happy Days Saloon. The delicious smell of grilled beef tacos and burritos filled his nose.

"Hey, it's the tiny cowboy poet," he said to himself as he looked down the veranda of the saloon. The little poet with the short legs and big hat sat back in his rocking chair and sang:

I like to smell the corn chips
I like to hear the bees
What I like to eat the most
Are beef tacos with peas

'Cause when I eat a taco
I also like a nacho
'cept when things go loco
And the nacho is too macho

What a funny song, Tuff thought.

"Sheriff Brunson, come quick," said a boy's voice as Tuff passed the Muleshoe jailhouse, which sat on Main Street next to the Happy Days. "We've got a big problem."

Tuff rounded the corner and looked toward the horse stables behind the jailhouse, where the voice seemed to come from. It sounded like a voice he knew.

"What the –?" Tuff said.

Outside the horse stables stood three people, dressed in white outfits. Tuff couldn't see their faces and hands, which were covered by masks and gloves.

"There's a problem in the stables," said the tallest masked person. "You need to come and see now."

Tuff didn't know who these three people in their strange outfits were but thought he had better make sure his horse Silver Heels was alright. He lowered his fingers to the bullwhip which hung from his star-studded belt and followed them as they kicked hay aside and walked into the stables.

As Tuff stepped inside, the smallest person quickly ran behind him and slammed the stable door shut. "Now," squealed a girl's voice.

Silver Heels whinnied, "Look out, Tuff."

He watched in horror as the remaining two masked people threw a saddle blanket aside. Underneath was a giant beehive. As soon as the blanket hit the ground the swarm spread out across the stables. The terrible sound of buzzing honeybees filled the air as they swooped and dove around Tuff's head. He knew no bullwhip could help him now.

"There's nowhere to hide, you bumbling sheriff," shouted the tallest masked person, who Tuff realized now was dressed like a

beekeeper. "Forty thousand honeybees will sting you. The only place you can escape is inside the jail."

Tuff knew the beekeeper was right. With his arm across his face to protect his eyes from the bees, he ran into the next building. He heard a door crash shut behind him. Tuff lowered his arm from his eyes and realized he was locked in one of his own jail cells.

The three beekeepers appeared outside the cell.

"Ha, ha," laughed the tallest as he took off his mask. "You fell for our trick."

It wasn't a beekeeper at all. Tuff stared into the nasty red eyes of "Big Nose" George Parrot, the meanest outlaw in the Wild West.

"Yeah," said the other two as they also took off their masks, gloves and white outfits. "It's 'Little Nose' George and 'Tiny Nose' Peggy, you dumb sheriff."

"We've got the sheriff locked in his own jail," said Big Nose George. "Now let's go have a delicious lunch at the Happy Days Saloon. After lunch we'll help ourselves to all the hideout kids' tooth fairy money."

"Then, for dessert, we'll come back and have big bowls of honey," said Tiny Nose Peggy.

"If you rob the kids, you're the ones who will get stung," said Tuff.

"Oh, so should we 'bee' careful?" said Big Nose George.

"Ha, ha, ha!" laughed The Parrot Gang as the three outlaws danced out of the jailhouse, slamming the door behind them.

CHAPTER TWO

SILVER HEELS TO THE RESCUE

How can I escape? Tuff thought. His deputy Sadie was doing a job for Judge June and wouldn't be able to hear him from here.

He remembered his big chestnut colt was in the stables right behind the jail. "Silver Heels," he called. "Get me out."

He waited and after a moment the door handle to the jail slowly started to turn. "Neigh!" He saw his trusted horse come in, licking his lips. "There's honey all over the door handle," Silver Heels whinnied, "delicious."

He handed Tuff the keys to the cell and Tuff was soon free. "Good boy." Tuff reached into his pocket. "Here, have an apple with your honey."

He led Silver Heels into the stable yard. "Now, Silver Heels, you stay here. I've got an idea about how to round up those Parrots."

Tuff picked up one of the white bee-protection outfits and put it on with the gloves and mask. *They won't guess who I am,* he thought.

Tuff ran back on to Main Street and pushed open the batwing doors to the Happy Days Saloon. "Hey, Big Nose George," Tuff said from behind his mask. "Your honeybees are escaping from the stables. You didn't shut the door."

"Let's get over there," shouted Big Nose George. "We can't let those bees escape."

The Parrot Gang raced back to the stables with Tuff close behind. He had left the door ajar and as soon as the gang were inside he stopped beside Silver Heels.

"Now," Tuff shouted and watched as the chestnut colt kicked the stable door shut, locking the Parrots inside with the bees.

"Hey, Parrots, your only escape is to run into the jail or you'll be stung by forty thousand bees," Tuff yelled through the door.

"Quick, duck into the jail," said Little Nose George. "I don't want to get stung."

Little Nose George is the dumbest outlaw ever, Tuff thought, as he ran into the jailhouse through its other door and locked the Parrots in a cell. Still in his protective outfit, he encouraged the remaining loose bees back into the stables, shut the door behind them and returned to the jailhouse.

"Well, I guess I'm the only one who'll get a taste of honey," Tuff laughed as the pandemonium of Parrots squawked inside the jail. "You three outlaws better bee-have. Crime doesn't pay."

"I see you've caught 'em again," smiled Judge Junia "June" Beak as she stepped into the jailhouse, looking for Tuff. "I was in my hut but heard what happened. They're just teenagers but those pretty Parrots have been in jail half their lives. They must like it in there."

"I still get my stars, don't I, Judge June?" Tuff asked.

"Of course," Judge June replied. "You get a gold star for your belt every time you capture an outlaw, even a joke of an outlaw like Big

Nose George. When the belt is filled, you'll be a US Marshall, top lawman in the West."

"We'll be out of here before you can say 'honeycomb'," growled Big Nose George. "This jail won't hold us for long."

"Sure, Parrot-Nose," laughed Judge June. "'Hive' a nice day. Try to 'bee' good."

"Yeah, try to stay sweet," Tuff laughed. He took off the beekeeper's outfit and put on his sheriff's hat.

"Leave Deputy Dan in charge," Judge June said. "He's just outside. I need you to come over to my hut. I've got an urgent job for you."

CHAPTER THREE

TROUBLE IN SOUTH TEXAS

Deputy Dan was asleep in his rocking chair on the veranda just outside the jailhouse. "Snore," he mumbled.

"I think I'll keep the cell keys with me," Tuff said. "He's just had his lunch, the usual four plates of burritos and tacos, so he'll be napping for a while."

He and Judge June started to cross the road. "Phew, what's that smell?" Tuff cried. "You're a disgusting rootin' tootin' deputy." Deputy Dan smiled in his sleep.

Tuff followed Judge June across Muleshoe's dusty Main Street. His eyes squinted under his wide-brimmed white hat toward the stream which trickled through the town. "Hi Mr. Zip," he said to his pet beaver as Mr. Zip ran up to join him.

"May I please have a honeybee lunch?" Mr. Zip asked.

"Of course, Mr. Zip," Tuff answered. "I haven't had my lunch either. We'll eat a little later but come with us now."

"What a polite pet you have, Tuff," said Judge June. "Not like mine."

Tuff and Mr. Zip followed Judge June into her hut. Tuff felt the cool breeze as she shut the door behind them.

"Hi Sadie. Hi Sawbones," said Tuff as he walked in. Deputy Sadie Marcus and Sawbones, Muleshoe's doctor, were standing in a corner of the hut next to a huge stuffed black bear with white teeth and sharp claws.

That bear always gives me the creeps, thought

Tuff. *Wait, did that claw just move?*

"Hey Tuff," said Sadie and Sawbones in unison. "Congrats on that bee-autiful capture of those pretty Parrots. Sorry we missed the action. Judge June had us on patrol around the outside of the town."

"Yeah, congrats, Sheriff," growled Wild Thing, Judge June's pet pink fairy armadillo. "Heard you got lucky. Where's my mash of honeybees? Huh? Huh?"

"Why can't you ask nicely, Wild Thing?" Mr. Zip said.

"'Cause I'm not a goody goody beaver like you," snarled Wild Thing. "Gimme my mash. NOW."

"Here you go, cutie-pie," Sadie said. "A bowl of fresh ground-up lizards. I know you like those too."

"CHOMP!" went Wild Thing. "TOOT!"

"Quiet everyone, listen up," said Judge June, waving a hand in front of her face. "I've had a message from Charlie 'Sir' Ringo down

17

in Matagorda in South Texas. He's moving a herd of five hundred longhorn cattle from Matagorda to Fort Worth."

"Charlie was a hideout kid. He used to live in Muleshoe," Tuff told Sawbones. "Is it the first time he's moved cattle on his own, as a cowboy?"

"Yes," answered Judge June. "The night they left Matagorda, Charlie thought they might have been followed and the next morning he was attacked by a nasty group of outlaws."

"Charlie's tough," said Tuff. "He used to guard our longhorns and goats when he lived here. That's how he got work as a cowboy."

"You're right," said Judge June. "But the outlaws stole fifty of his cattle. He finally fought them off but needs help in case they attack again."

"I hope it's not The Nacho Gang," said Sawbones. "Before I became a hideout kid, I saw them run with my old boss Sam Bass and his gang. They're ruthless."

"You're right, Sawbones," said Sadie as she glanced at him with her deep black eyes. "They're the fiercest cattle rustlers in South Texas. I've read about them in the magazine, *This Week in the Wild West*."

Judge June said, "I'm not sure which gang it is. Your job is to ride down to South Texas, meet Charlie and help him get the herd of longhorns up to Fort Worth. You think you can handle the outlaws?"

"Better take me," Wild Thing growled. "I love to eat nachos with extra cheese and chili peppers."

"No," said Judge June. "Your toots will be worse than normal."

"Like this?" Wild Thing laughed as she let loose a massive armadillo toot that seemed fifty times her size. The smell of the toot filled the room.

"That's disgusting," said Mr. Zip, coughing. "Your toots are bigger than a cow's."

"We can handle the outlaws," said Tuff, keeping one hand over his nose and lowering the other to his bullwhip. "Sadie, Sawbones and I will get started in the morning."

"I'm afraid the morning is too late," Judge June said. "Charlie needs your help right away or he might lose his entire herd. You'll leave as soon as you've had some lunch. Now close your eyes very tightly and don't say a word."

Judge June, the good witch, raised her arms toward the sky and quietly chanted a spell. A cool breeze filled the hut.

"You may open your eyes now," said Judge June.

The Deputies looked at one another. They knew the witch's spell would help them with their mission.

Judge June gazed at them with her almond-shaped blue-gray eyes. "Remember," she said, "it's easier to *stay* out of trouble than to *get* out of trouble. Be careful."

CHAPTER FOUR

THE DASH DOWN THE COLORADO RIVER TRAIL

After a quick lunch in the Happy Days Saloon, Tuff led Sadie and Sawbones into the stables. They were greeted by the sound of honeybees quietly humming in their hive.

"What should we do with the beehive?" Sadie asked. "We can't just leave the bees in the stables while we go off to South Texas."

"How about we throw the hive into the jail cell with The Parrot Gang?" laughed Sawbones. "They could eat honeybees for a few days. Or the honeybees could eat them."

"Probably not a good idea," said Tuff. He tossed one of Silver Heels' extra saddle blankets over the hive. "That should keep them calm until we get back."

Tuff, Sadie and Sawbones packed up their saddlebags with their bedrolls and cans of beans. "What have you got there, Sadie?" Tuff asked. "That looks like a fiddle case."

"It's Toothless Tom's violin. I've borrowed it," said Sadie. "We might want to sing around the campfire."

"He doesn't know you've borrowed it, does he Sadie?" Tuff scolded.

"These honeybees are making me nervous. Let's get moving," Sadie said, ignoring Tuff.

Sadie hopped up on Jenny, her big mare, and Tuff mounted Silver Heels. As soon as Sawbones stuck his boots in his gray colt Jack's stirrups, they galloped out of the stables and away from Muleshoe.

*

"I checked the map," Tuff said as the three Deputies rode through Horsehead Canyon. "We follow the Colorado River all the way from Muleshoe to South Texas. We should meet Charlie 'Sir' Ringo tomorrow around lunchtime, near the town of La Grange. Let's make camp soon."

The hot June sun slowly dropped below the horizon. Soon a bright summer moon lit the landscape. The Deputies saw white-tailed deer scamper away as they rode past the prickly pear cacti along the Colorado River Trail.

As Tuff asked, "Are you OK riding in the dark, Sawbones?" he saw Jack suddenly stop and raise his front legs high in the air, almost throwing Sawbones out of the saddle.

"What is it?" cried Sadie. Jenny was snorting and stomping the ground.

Tuff peered ahead and whispered, "Quiet. Just in front of us is a sounder of wild razorback hogs. Their tusks can rip a horse's legs wide open."

"GRUNT! GRUNT!" The sound of the snuffling hogs filled the air.

"Man, do they stink," muttered Sawbones. "And even with my one eye, they sure look ugly."

Sawbones stared into the gloom with his left eye. An eyepatch covered his right one.

Tuff trotted close enough to the hogs to get his bullwhip within range.

I've never used this whip on hogs before. Hope it works.

"CRACK!"

"Move on out, you dirty razorbacks, or we'll make bacon out of you."

Silver Heels snorted as Tuff rode forward and whipped the razorback herd away from the river and up into a canyon.

"Nice work, Tuff," Sadie said.

"Thanks. Let's bed down here for the night," Tuff said. "It's sheltered now with the hogs gone. The horses have lots of water. We'll have a fast ride tomorrow morning."

"I'm glad Judge June made you a deputy," Tuff said to Sawbones as they gathered firewood and made a supper of beans and turkey sausages. "When you left Sam Bass's gang and came on the right side of the law, you made the right choice. Do you miss the outlaw life?"

"Not at all," said Sawbones. "Now I get to use my doctor skills on the good guys."

"What about The Nacho Gang, Sawbones?" Sadie said. "Are they as mean as we've heard?"

"Even Sam Bass was afraid of them," said Sawbones. "When they rustle cattle, they don't like to leave any witnesses."

Sadie shuddered. "I hope it's not them rustling Charlie's longhorns."

"Shhh, quiet," Tuff breathed. "What's that noise? Coyotes?"

The shrill yelp of a band of prairie wolves cut through the night. "Those howls give me the creeps," said Sadie.

The howls stopped. The three Deputies strained to hear a different sound, a faint shuffling noise like someone stepping on twigs.

"Let's sleep with one eye open tonight," Tuff said. "We're already close to cattle-rustling country."

CHAPTER FIVE

THE COWBOY

CHARLIE "SIR" RINGO

The Deputies woke at dawn to the sound of mourning doves and their familiar song of "Hoo-hoo, hoo, hoo, hoo."

"Today's another scorcher," Tuff said as they packed up their saddlebags after a quick breakfast of apple juice, onions, beans and toast. "Better make sure we give the horses plenty of water. Hey, did either of you notice someone creeping nearby last night?"

"I thought I did," said Sadie.

31

They mounted up and continued down the river trail as fast as they could.

After stopping to water the horses near the town of Austin, they came to a bend in the river.

"Somewhere along here should be the low water crossing where Charlie 'Sir' Ringo can lead his longhorns across the Colorado River," said Tuff.

"Look, there they are," Sadie shouted, pointing into the distance. "I see Charlie."

A huge cloud of dust rose from the ground as a herd of longhorns walked slowly toward the river.

"MOO!" bellowed the cattle.

The three Deputies slowed their horses and crossed the river to meet the Trail Drive. They trotted up to Charlie, who was joined by two of his cowboys, also on horseback.

"Tuff," exclaimed Charlie. "Man, am I glad to see you. Outlaw rustlers attacked. They've already stolen fifty steers. Howdy

Sadie, who's your friend?"

"This is Joe Newton. Also known as Sawbones."

"Nice to meet you, Sawbones. Welcome to rustler country."

Tuff had never seen Charlie look so ragged. He was covered from head to toe with dust and his chaps and broad-brimmed hat were caked with mud. Even his horse, Colonel Clop, looked like an old workhorse.

"You look like a real cowboy," Tuff said. "So you're the Trail Boss for the first time?"

"YIPPEE-YAY!"

"There's a rustler," Charlie yelled, pointing at the edge of the herd. A dark figure galloped through the cattle, trying to separate three of the cows from the rest.

"I'll get him," Sadie said as she urged Jenny forward.

Tuff watched, amazed, as the big mare flew across the ground. Sadie quickly wrapped her whip around the rustler, stopping him, before trotting back with the thief behind on his horse.

"Wow," Charlie said with a smile as Sadie rode up. "You've got one fast horse there, Sadie."

"I had a little help from our boss back in Muleshoe," Sadie said, winking at Tuff and Sawbones.

Charlie turned to the rustler. "Now listen up you filthy outlaw. Tell me who you work for."

The outlaw stared off into the distance and whined, "You hurt my arm when you bullwhipped me."

"Talk to us, cattle thief," Sadie said, "or the next wrap-up will hurt a lot more."

"I work for The Nacho Gang," hissed the outlaw. "We're gonna take all your cattle. Ha, ha, ha."

The Nacho Gang, thought Tuff. *Oh dear.*

CHAPTER SIX

LA GRANGE

"Put this rustler on one of the extra ponies," Charlie told his cowboys. "He can trail behind the herd. Somebody should look at his arm."

"We have a doctor right here," Tuff said. "You have to work on bad guys after all, Sawbones."

"Yeah, I'll have a look at him," Sawbones said, checking the outlaw's arm and applying a bandage.

"Sawbones used to ride with Sam Bass and his gang," Tuff said to Charlie. "But he came

over to our side and Judge June made him a deputy."

"Sam Bass," said Charlie. "He's almost as dangerous as The Nacho Gang."

"Even Sam was scared of the Nachos," said Sawbones. "Especially the leader, 'Macho' Nacho."

"Let's get these cattle moving," Charlie shouted to his cowboys. "We can make it to the town of La Grange by nightfall. There's plenty of free water and grass there."

Tuff and Sadie rode with Charlie as the

cowboys whistled and whooped the herd across the Colorado River. Sawbones kept an eye on the rustler at the rear.

"I like your cattle brand, Charlie," said Sadie, as she looked at a nearby steer. "How do you do the branding?"

"Like every other cattle owner, I use a branding iron. It's put in a red-hot fire then placed on their hide for five seconds. That's how I know which cattle belong to me," Charlie said.

"So if these cattle are stolen by a rustler, and the rustler tries to sell them, the buyer should know they are your cattle," said Sadie.

"Exactly," said Charlie. "The outlaws will try to sell the herd but hopefully the buyer will beware and not pay for them."

"Crime doesn't pay," said Sadie with a smile. She glanced at the bar hanging from Charlie's saddle. "Is that your branding iron?"

"It is," Charlie replied. "I carry it with me everywhere. There was only one time when an outlaw stole it from me. But I soon got it back."

"Hey," said Tuff. "There's the sign for La Grange."

LA GRANGE
Plenty of FREE water and grass for yor cattle!

Cattle rustlers NOT welcum

ONE MILE AHED ↑

"Great," said Sadie. "Can we make the saloon in La Grange our first stop? I'm dying for a sarsaparilla."

Sawbones rode up to join them. "That outlaw will be OK. And he told me Macho Nacho is not with his gang right now – he's miles away."

"OK, Sawbones, that's good to know." Charlie shouted to the cowboys, "Get these steers over to the grazing pasture and set yourselves up all around them as herd-riding guards. We'll be in the saloon in town. Come get me right away if there's trouble."

Charlie led the way as he, Tuff, Sadie and Sawbones galloped the short distance into La Grange. The town bustled with horses, cattle and people.

"Something's very strange about this town," Tuff said as they rode past the General Store. "Every single person looks like an outlaw. Dirty black hats and red eyes."

They tied up their horses outside the Fat Pig Saloon. Sawbones had a worried look on his face. "What is it, Sawbones?" Tuff asked.

"I think I recognize some of these people,"

answered Sawbones. "Scary faces are hard to forget. These guys look like the outlaws who ride with The Nacho Gang. At least we

won't have to worry about Macho Nacho, though."

The three Deputies and Charlie pushed open the batwing doors and strode into the noisy saloon.

The noise stopped the instant the batwings shuttered closed. A crowd of ornery cowboys surrounded them. It was deathly silent.

A lone cowboy at the bar turned around on his stool and stared hard at Tuff.

"Welcome to La Grange, Sheriff Brunson. I see you brought your sidekick Deputy Marcus with you. Is that your doctor, Sawbones? Of course I recognize Charlie 'Sir' Ringo." The cowboy stared directly at them. "I was expecting you. My name is Guillermo. But most people call me Macho."

Tuff drew in a breath.

"Macho Nacho."

CHAPTER SEVEN

MACHO NACHO

Tuff glanced at Charlie and Sadie. He saw complete fear in their eyes.

"Yeah well, we're not looking for trouble, *Señor* Nacho," said Tuff. "We're passing through town with Charlie's herd of longhorns. We'll be gone tomorrow."

"Ha, ha, ha!" laughed Macho Nacho as all the outlaws laughed with him. "You sure will."

Macho Nacho hopped down off his bar stool and walked toward them.

"He's the shortest, widest outlaw I've ever

seen," Tuff whispered to Sadie. "He looks like a steer."

"So you think I look like a cow?" Macho Nacho stopped and shouted. "Maybe you can tell me how *this* happened."

Tuff watched, horrified, as Macho Nacho took off his dark, stained shirt and turned around.

In the middle of his bare back was the black outline of a brand. *Oh no*, Tuff thought, *it's Charlie's brand, the same one he uses to brand his longhorns.*

"As you can see I was branded by your friend Charlie 'Sir' Ringo. Just as if I was a cow, who belonged to him," Macho Nacho said, with a voice like low thunder. "I've been waiting to take my revenge on Charlie 'Sir' Ringo."

Tuff thought fast. "But Charlie would never do that to you, *Señor* Nacho. He's always on the right side of the law, like us. His brand was stolen from him a while ago by an outlaw. That outlaw must be the guy you're after."

47

"That outlaw was working for Charlie," shouted Macho Nacho. "He told me that."

Tuff decided not to argue, for now. "You said you were expecting us. How did you know we were coming here?" he asked.

"We've followed you since you left Muleshoe, Sheriff," said Macho Nacho. "I've got a spy on the trail who told me you were heading this way. You were lucky those razorbacks didn't cut up your horses."

"What do you want from us?" Tuff asked. "We haven't done you any harm."

"The town of La Grange belongs to us. To leave, you have to pay us."

"Pay you?" said Tuff. "The grazing around La Grange is free range. It's free for all of the herds."

"Maybe you didn't hear me, Sheriff Brunson," Macho Nacho snapped. "As of today, the town belongs to The Nacho Gang. For you and your Deputies to leave, you'll have to pay *us*."

Sadie whispered, "Maybe we should just pay him, Tuff. Not worth the trouble."

"Not worth the trouble?" Macho Nacho shouted. "You might not have noticed Deputy Marcus but I can hear every word you say."

"OK, *Señor* Nacho," Tuff said. "How much do you want?"

"Not much at all," said Macho Nacho with an evil smile. "Here's what I want: You can give us every single longhorn in Charlie's herd. You can give us all your horses."

49

Tuff heard boots shuffling as the outlaw gang surrounded them.

"And you can leave Charlie 'Sir' Ringo with me," Macho Nacho said quietly. "Me and him have some settling up to do."

"We need some time to think about this, *Señor* Nacho," Tuff said.

"OK Sheriff, how about thirty seconds," said Macho Nacho, laughing.

"Ha, ha, ha," laughed all the outlaws with him. "Ha, ha, ha," Tuff heard the outlaws' horses whinny from outside the saloon.

"I tell you what," said Macho Nacho. "I'll give you one hour to decide. After that, you either pay up or *else*."

"Will you leave us here to discuss it on our own?" Tuff asked.

"Sure," said Macho Nacho. "On your own – with my head cowboy keeping watch on you. Oh, here he comes now."

"POW!" The saloon batwing doors slammed open. The biggest outlaw Tuff had ever seen rumbled into the saloon.

"Say hello to 'Gigante'," roared Macho Nacho. "He'll keep order while you're deciding whether to pay up, or *else*."

I wonder just what "or else" means? Tuff thought.

"*Vamos chicos*; let's go boys," Macho Nacho said to his outlaws and all of them except Gigante left the Fat Pig Saloon.

CHAPTER EIGHT

GIGANTE

Tuff gathered Sadie, Charlie and Sawbones around him. They sat down at a table in a corner of the dark saloon. He glanced over at Gigante, who ordered a cactus juice at the bar.

"I'm worried," Tuff said. "I've never seen an outlaw as angry as Macho Nacho. He wants revenge on Charlie, even though he's wrong about him. Charlie, do you have any idea who stole your branding iron?"

Charlie looked down at the floor, then raised his eyes and said in a whisper, "I do. There were three outlaws that jumped me back in Matagorda. Two I could see; they were just the usual filthy outlaws. But one came up behind me and pinned my arms back while they took my branding iron. He was big and very strong. The two in front of me called him 'Gigante'."

"Could it be the same Gigante?" said Tuff, looking at the giant at the bar. "You didn't see him?"

"No," answered Charlie. "But he said something very strange. While he had my arms pinned Gigante whispered, 'Don't worry, Charlie, you'll get your branding iron back. I just need it for a few hours.'"

"Why would Gigante want to steal Charlie's branding iron and use it to brand Macho Nacho?" Sadie asked.

"Because I want to take over Macho's gang," said Gigante. He had left the bar and now towered over their table. The Deputies and Charlie almost jumped out of their boots.

"Everyone thinks because I'm a giant

I'm very dumb," said Gigante. A small tear trickled down his cheek. "The truth is I'm tired of the outlaw life. Macho Nacho is nothing but a bully, picking on everyone."

"But everyone says he is so mean and not scared of anything," Sadie said.

"Not scared?" laughed Gigante. "He's scared to death of one thing."

"What's that?" Tuff asked.

"Bullwhips," said Gigante. "Now that he has a brand on his back, Macho thinks he is a bull. Bulls hate bullwhips. They are always getting roped, lashed and tied up by cowboys and their whips."

"Is that why he can hear so well?" asked Sadie. "Bulls have a strong sense of hearing."

"Exactly," said Gigante. "Once the brand seared his back, he became like a bull. Even more mean and nasty, with great hearing, but he can't see very well. He even looks like a bull."

"And smells like one too," said Sawbones.

"I had to use your branding iron, Charlie. I knew Macho Nacho would come after you when he found out it was your brand and Sheriff Tuff and Deputy Sadie would be sent here to help you. You're all hideout kids. Hideout kids stick together. Sheriff Brunson," said Gigante as he nodded toward Tuff, "you have the reputation as the most magical in all of Texas with your bullwhip. Since you are Charlie's friend, I knew you would come to protect him."

"Wow, that's a very clever idea, Gigante," said Tuff. "And if you take over Macho's gang, then you can choose to be on the right side of the law. An ex-outlaw."

Tuff thought for a moment.

"I've got a plan for how we can trick Macho Nacho. Gather around everybody."

Tuff drew out a piece of parchment and sketched his plan on it with a quill pen, carefully pointing out what everyone should do. Then he put the parchment back in his pocket, straightened up and shouted, "Hey Macho Nacho, come on in. We're ready to pay up."

Tuff expected to see the batwing doors fly open. Instead there was only silence.

He waited a few more seconds.

"I wonder where he is?" he said to Charlie.

Charlie shrugged. "Here, Gigante, take this extra bullwhip. I always keep one handy."

Charlie, Sawbones, Sadie and Gigante all got behind Tuff as he crept toward the batwing doors. They had their fingers on their bullwhips ready to strike.

Tuff drew in a breath and pushed the doors open.

"What the -?"

He looked outside.

The town was empty.

CHAPTER NINE

THE BATTLE FOR CHARLIE'S LONGHORNS

"There's nobody in sight," Tuff said.

"Oh no," cried Sadie, joining Tuff in the saloon doorway. "Our horses are gone. Silver Heels, Jenny, Jack and Colonel Clop have been stolen by Macho Nacho."

"That outlaw didn't wait for an answer," said Tuff. "He took our horses. I bet he'll try to run off with the herd."

"Quick, come with me," said Gigante.

The Deputies and Charlie followed Gigante as he ran behind the saloon and up to a barn. The giant opened a wooden door and they peered into the dark. "Smells like horses," said Sawbones.

Gigante threw open a window and the Texas sunlight shone on five beautiful Spanish ponies.

"My secret supply of fast ponies," said Gigante. "I keep 'em hidden in here."

"Neigh," whinnied the Spanish ponies. "*Hola.*"

"Let's hop on," said Tuff as he gritted his teeth. "Time to ride out and whip Macho Nacho into shape. *Nobody* steals Silver Heels and gets away with it."

They mounted the fast horses and breezed out of La Grange to the grasslands. Tuff slowed to a trot. "There they are," he said, pointing to Charlie's longhorns a little way ahead.

Macho Nacho and his gang circled the

herd, turning them away from La Grange. The outlaw leader was astride Silver Heels.

"He's got my cowboys tied up," said Charlie. "They're all sitting in the chuck wagon. The outlaw we captured earlier is guarding them."

"Everybody ready?" Tuff said. "Let's ride. You lead the way, Gigante."

"Macho," hollered Gigante, as he rode toward the outlaw leader. "The sheriff and his deputies have found my Spanish ponies and they're behind me. They've got their bullwhips out."

"Oh no," yelled Macho Nacho. "Bullwhips. Let's get out of here."

Tuff closed his eyes. *Please work this time,* he thought. "Look out you dirty outlaw. Here comes Sheriff Tuff Brunson!"

"CRACK!"

Tuff opened his eyes. His whip was wrapped around the head outlaw. He yanked Macho Nacho off Silver Heels. Charlie and the others rounded up their horses as the outlaws who had been riding them fled into some nearby live oak trees.

"You were wrong about me, Macho," Charlie said as he and Gigante joined Tuff. "Tell him, Gigante."

"I was the one who branded you," Gigante said to his former boss. "I'm tired of you bullying hard-working Trail Drivers and rustling cattle that don't belong to you. I knew that if he thought Charlie was in trouble, Sheriff Brunson would come and help me catch you."

"You're finished as an outlaw, *Señor* Macho," Tuff said. "Let's get this horn-less bull tied up and take him to jail."

"Crime doesn't pay, Macho," said Sadie as she patted her horse Jenny. "Good girl," she whispered. "I hope the outlaws weren't mean to you. Here's an apple."

"I'm gonna get you, Gigante," bleated Macho as he looked up from where he lay on the dusty pasture. "My revenge will be sweet.

Hey, get me off the ground. I'm covered in fire ants. Ouch!"

After untying Charlie's cowboys, Tuff and his two deputies roped Macho Nacho tightly and put him in the chuck wagon instead.

"Let's calm these cattle," Charlie ordered. "WHOOP! WHOOP!"

The longhorn herd followed the cattle call and slowly gathered together. The Trail Drive was underway again, with Gigante alongside.

Tuff, Charlie, Sawbones and Sadie led the way as they lazily moved up the dusty trail along Owl Creek.

"We can drop Macho Nacho at the jailhouse in the town of Dime Box," said Tuff. "The sheriff there is a friend of mine."

"It's almost sunset," Charlie said, "Let's make camp here for the night. It's got water and good grass."

Silver Heels' ears pricked up as they came over a small hill.

"Whoa," Tuff said.

A loud flutter of wings came from up ahead. "BEAT! BEAT!" Dozens of small gray birds took flight.

"Look," said Sadie. "It's a big covey of quail. I wonder what spooked them?"

They made supper and the cowboys rounded up the cattle in the tall grass for the night. Tuff wished everyone goodnight as they crawled into their bedrolls.

"Tuff," whispered Sadie. "What was that noise?"

"MOO! MOO!" bellowed the cattle.

"Something is stirring up those steers," said Charlie, sitting up.

"MOO! MOO!" came an even louder call from the steers.

"Look," said Sadie. "Those eyes."

The campers looked where Sadie was pointing. Glowing in the darkness was a huge pair of yellow cat's eyes.

"Panther," yelled Charlie, leaping out of

his bedroll. "Watch out for the herd."

It was too late. The sound of thundering hooves echoed from the ground as the longhorns raced away from the growling, snarling panther.

"Stampede," yelled Charlie. "Get on your horses, quick."

The full summer moon shone down on them and Charlie's cowboys as they mounted up and whooped at the herd trying to contain it. The cattle all ran in one direction, behind the lead steer, but they couldn't be stopped.

"I've got it," cried Sadie. "My fiddle. Cattle can be calmed by the sound of a violin and singing."

Sadie reached inside her saddlebag and grabbed the violin from its case. She started playing as loudly as she could. The cowboys joined in singing, "Dinah Had a Wooden Leg" and "Cotton-Eyed Joe".

"Get up near the lead steer, Old Blue,"

Charlie shouted to Sadie. "If you can slow him down the rest will follow."

Sadie spurred Jenny and rode with one hand while she cradled the violin in her neck and played with the other. *How can you play the violin with only one hand?* Tuff wondered.

Right ahead of Sadie was a ditch in the pasture. "Look out," Tuff called.

Too late. Sadie rode into the ditch and the stampeding cattle almost knocked her off Jenny.

Sadie held on and wrapped her left leg around Jenny's saddle. Her right leg trailed on the ground. "I'm riding side-saddle," she yelled to Tuff as she rode out of the ditch.

"C'mon, Sadie," shouted Tuff. "You can do it."

Sadie was nearly at the front of the herd. She took Jenny's reins between her teeth and, with the violin in her other hand, grabbed her bullwhip. She snapped it over Old Blue's head.

"CRACK!" She snapped her whip again.

Old Blue came to a stop and the stampede slowed behind him. Sadie played the violin again and gradually all the cattle stopped and listened to the sweet songs.

How did she do that? wondered Tuff. Only *Judge June could have made that happen.*

He looked around to see if everything was alright now.

"Watch out," Tuff shouted. "The stampede opened the wagon. Macho Nacho is trying to get away."

Tuff urged Silver Heels on after the escaping bandit thinking, *Just hold the reins tightly and make sure he doesn't get away.*

"Look out you dirty outlaw. Here comes Sheriff Tuff Brunson!"

"CRACK!"

Tuff snapped his whip and once again, Macho Nacho fell whimpering to the ground.

"Where did that panther get to?" Sawbones yelled. "There he goes. I've got him."

Tuff watched as Sawbones galloped across the dark pasture on Jack.

"CRACK!"

Sawbones' bullwhip wound around the panther's neck and the big cat hit the dirt.

"Quick, help us get the panther under control," Tuff called out to Charlie's cowboys as the panther's paws thrashed the ground and he tried to get free of the whip. A couple of them rode across and helped tie the panther safely under a tree. Macho Nacho was still wrapped up in Tuff's bullwhip and Tuff and Sawbones loaded him back in the chuck wagon.

"Nice work," Tuff said as Sadie rode up with the fiddle tucked under her arm. "Good idea to bring the violin, even though it doesn't belong to you. What if you broke it?"

"Why don't you mind your own business?" Sadie smiled. "But I don't think I should play anymore. None of these cowboys can sing. They sounded like screeching owls."

"Whew, what a night," said Charlie. "We need a big drink of sarsaparilla to help us sleep. We can start for Fort Worth in the morning."

'Do you mind if I come with you, Charlie?" asked Gigante. "I've got family in Fort Worth. I'd like to settle there. I don't want to take over The Nacho gang anymore – too many bad eggs in that crowd."

"I don't mind one bit, Gigante."

They rode back to their camp and, after Charlie had given everyone a drink of sarsaparilla, Tuff hopped back in his bedroll. Just as he nodded off he thought, *We were lucky to capture Macho Nacho. I hope he's in jail for a long time.*

.

CHAPTER TEN

A "SWEET" ENDING

Tuff woke to the sound of crickets chirping in the South Texas morning. A lone mockingbird sang the song of a white-winged dove. Tuff loved the Texas mockingbirds, which imitated or "mocked" the songs of other birds.

"How about that stampede last night?" he said to Sadie and Charlie with a yawn. "Just when we thought we had things under control with The Nacho Gang, up pops a panther."

"That's the way it goes on Trail Drives," said

Charlie. "It's one thing after another. You have to manage three of the wildest beasts in the animal kingdom: horses, cattle and cowboys."

"Sadie and I will take Macho Nacho over to Dime Box and drop him off at the jailhouse," Tuff told him. "My sheriff friend there will lock him up and throw away the key."

Tuff and Sadie mounted their horses and put the tied-up Macho Nacho across Jack's back. "We'll see you on the road to Fort Worth," Tuff said as they rode out of the camp to the little town of Dime Box. It was only a short distance away.

The sheriff met them outside the jailhouse.

"Thanks Sheriff," Tuff said, as they turned

the outlaw over to him. "He's the nastiest outlaw we've ever met. In the Wild West the worst thing you can do is to steal someone's horse. Even most outlaws won't ever do that," said Tuff.

The sheriff shook Tuff's hand and threw Macho Nacho in jail.

Tuff and Sadie rejoined Sawbones, Charlie, his cowboys and Gigante further along the trail. It was early evening and low thunder rolled gently across the flat plains. Flashes of midsummer lightning lit up the western sky and, in front of them, a sign appeared.

"This is where Sadie, Sawbones and I leave you," said Tuff. "Great to have met you, Gigante." Tuff shook their new friend's hand then turned to say goodbye to Charlie. "Good luck, cowboy. Happy trails."

"Thanks friends, I couldn't have made it without you. Hideout kids stick together," Charlie said with a broad grin. "C'mon, Gigante."

"Bye, Tuff. Bye, Sadie and Sawbones. Hope to see you again. Crime doesn't pay," Gigante said with a big smile as he and Charlie rode off with the herd.

"Let's ride," Tuff said and he, Sadie and Sawbones fairly flew west on the Goodnight-Loving Trail back to Muleshoe.

A few hours later they arrived at the Happy Days Saloon, where Judge June waited on the veranda.

"Welcome home." Judge June smiled as they dismounted and joined her inside for a sarsaparilla. "I got a message from Charlie

'Sir' Ringo. He filled me in on a bit of trouble you had with *Señor* Macho Nacho. Now *he* sounds like someone who needs to spend the rest of his days behind bars."

"And nights. But I'm not sure he was the scariest part of the job," Tuff said. "The stampede was terrifying. Luckily Sadie had brought along a violin. She managed to calm down Old Blue, the leader of the herd."

Judge June smiled a mysterious smile. "I see," she said. "Good job, Sadie."

"So you're the one who had it," said Toothless Tom, the bartender. He took the instrument from Sadie. "I've been looking for my violin everywhere."

"What about Big Nose George and his flock of Parrots?" Sawbones asked. "Do they need a doctor? Perhaps they have a few bee stings?"

Judge June laughed. "You can see for yourself." She led them to the jailhouse.

Tuff couldn't believe his eyes as they

walked in. The Parrots were gone.

"Don't worry," said Judge June. "Come with me to the stables."

They followed her. Inside the stables all three Parrots sat on a wooden bench. They spooned big heaps of honey into shiny glass jars, then screwed caps on to the jars.

Labels on the jars read: "Parrot Honey: Made from Muleshoe honeybees by the Parrot Family. We're not sweet but our honey is."

"You've tamed the wild beasts," Tuff exclaimed. "Have they really learned crime doesn't pay?"

"No," said Judge June. "Look behind them."

The Parrots were tied down to the bench with thick ropes. And behind the ropes sat Mr. Zip and Wild Thing. They had their teeth bared as they gulped bites of honey.

"We're guarding these Parrots," Wild Thing growled. "We'll bite 'em if they try to escape."

"Yeah," Mr. Zip said. "We're big and strong now after all this honey."

"I've told the Parrots that if they are able to make a million jars of honey I'll let them out of jail one day earlier," Judge June said.

"Ha!" laughed Tuff. "It sounds like a sweet deal to me."

THE END

AUTHOR'S NOTE

The Hideout Kids series of books feature several of the same characters, animals, places and things. Here are some brief descriptions:

Charlie "Sir" Ringo: A cowboy detective.

Deputy Joe "Sawbones" Newton: Muleshoe's doctor, a deputy to Sheriff Tuff Brunson.

Deputy Sadie Marcus: Ten-year-old deputy of Muleshoe and Tuff's best friend.

Hooter: Judge June's familiar. An owl-shaped spirit who helps Judge June practice her magic.

Jack: Sawbones' horse.

Jelly Roll Jim, Toothless Tom, Deputy Dan Pigeon: Teenagers who grew up in Muleshoe and stayed on to help Judge June and the hideout kids.

Jenny: Sadie's horse. A gift from Chief Ten Bears of the Comanche Tribe Indians.

Judge Junia "June" Beak: United States District Judge of the West. She is also a good and powerful witch.

Miss Hannah Humblebee: A Hopi Tribe Indian girl detective.

Mr. Zip: Tuff's pet. A beaver.

Muleshoe, Texas: Home of the hideout kids. Only children can find it and live there.

S'mores: Chocolate-covered marshmallows, served on sugar crackers. Dee-lish.

Sarsaparilla: The most popular soft drink of the Wild West. It's thought to have healing powers and is made from the root of the sarsaparilla vine. Yummy.

Sheriff Tuff Brunson: Ten-year-old sheriff of Muleshoe.

Silver Heels: Tuff's horse. Also a gift from Chief Ten Bears.

Spiky: A giant saguaro cactus that guards The Cave.

The Cave: A magical place where the kids can travel through time.

The Singing Cowboy Poet: A magical elf.

Wild Thing: Judge June's pet. A pink fairy armadillo.

Here are descriptions of a few animals and plants which you might not have seen before, and which appear in this book:

Covey: A group of quail.

Coyote: A wild prairie wolf.

Live oak trees: A typical tree of Texas. They stay green throughout the year thus are known as "live" oaks.

Mesquite trees: Typical tree of the Texas desert.

Sounder: A group of hogs.

Coming Soon from the Hideout Kids

THE PARROT GANG & WILD WEST GHOSTS

Chapter One

SHOWDOWN AT THE HAPPY DAYS SALOON

A cold winter wind swirled down dusty Main Street in Muleshoe, Texas. It was the last day of December, New Year's Eve. Sheriff Tuff Brunson wrapped his buckskin coat around his shoulders as he and Deputy Sadie Marcus patrolled the street on their horses Silver

Heels and Jenny. Hope there's no trouble today, he thought. It's been a pretty good year.

"If this wind gets any stronger it might blow us to the next town," Tuff said as he looked over at Sadie. Her black ponytails blew straight back. "Let's duck into the Happy Days Saloon for a hot sarsaparilla."

"It's too windy to keep our hats on," Sadie said as they tied up their horses, grabbed their broad-brimmed white hats in their hands and hurried off the street.

As Tuff led the way up the steps to the saloon a small figure on the veranda caught his eye. "Look, Sadie, it's the singing cowboy poet," he whispered.

As usual the tiny cowboy was rocking in his old wooden rocking chair. He sang:

When Tuff & Sadie arrived
In this pretty town
Big Nose George was king
And claimed the outlaw crown

The pack of Parrots nest
In their red tree house
But when the ghosts show up
They'll hide like a mouse

"Let's go in, Tuff," Sadie said with a shiver. "I don't like songs about ghosts." They pushed through the batwing doors into the Happy Days.

"Where is everybody?" Tuff asked in a quiet voice. The four wooden tables and the few stools at the shiny wooden bar were empty. The smell of delicious s'mores was absent.

"I wondered that myself," Sadie replied. "Let's look around."

"Even Toothless Tom, the bartender, has wandered off," Tuff said. "This is strange. It's New Year's Eve. There should be a big party. But we've got it to ourselves."

"No you don't, Sheriff," a gruff voice said from the far corner of the room.

Boots shuffled on the wooden floor. Outlaws in black hats and red bandanas appeared from dark corners.

"What the –?" Tuff said.

"Pop, pop, pop," went the sound of bubblegum exploding from outlaw mouths.

"Nice of you to drop in. You remember me, don't you?" said "Big Nose" George Parrot, the meanest outlaw in the West, as he walked toward Tuff. "My brother 'Little Nose' George is here too. Ha, ha, ha."

"Ha, ha, ha. Thanks for droppin' in," sneered Little Nose George.

"Yeah, I remember you," said Tuff. "I might forget a face. But I never forget a smell, especially one as bad as yours. You smell like a rotten catfish. You must be one of those teenagers who has a bath once every ten years."

"Not funny," yelled Big Nose George. He glared at his sister, "Tiny Nose" Peggy, as she snickered behind him. "Stop gigglin', Peggy."

"Sorry," she said, still giggling.

"Yeah, don't laugh, Tiny Nose Peggy," said Sadie. "You smell even worse than your big brother."

"Grrr -" said Tiny Nose Peggy. "Let me pop her on the head. I wanna, I wanna, I wanna."

"What are you doing here, Parrots?" Tuff demanded. "Muleshoe is a kids-only town. No teenage outlaws allowed."

"Uh, I guess I forgot," said Big Nose George. "Now you listen up. I've got my sidekick with me, 'Short Arm' Sam. His finger gets real twitchy 'cause his arm is too short so don't try anythin' funny. He'll bash you if he can reach you. Ha, ha, ha."

Tuff saw "Short Arm" Sam standing in the corner and thought, *Boy, is he ugly.*

"Ha, ha, ha," giggled Little Nose George.

"Your brain must be the same size as your nose," Tuff said to Little Nose George. "All you can do is copy your brother."

"Shut up, Sheriff," shouted Big Nose George. "I know my little brother's brain is the size of a pea but I'll be doin' the talkin' around here. All you and Deputy Ponytails got is a couple of bullwhips. But there ain't no bulls around here, just outlaws."

"Ha, ha, ha," laughed Little Nose George and Tiny Nose Peggy.

"Now, Dep-u-ties," said Big Nose George, "since you're nice and quiet, here's a last chance for you."

"A what?" Tuff said.

"A last chance. This is it." Big Nose George pulled out his super soaker water gun. "Get your hands in the air."

MIKE GLEASON

HIDEOUT KIDS

TUFF, SADIE
& THE WILD WEST

MIKE GLEASON

HIDEOUT KIDS

GENERAL MUSTER
& NO-TREES TOWN

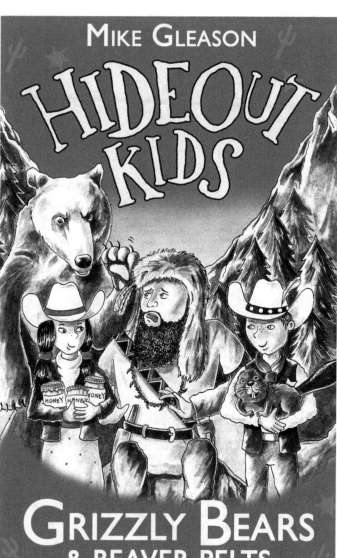

MIKE GLEASON

HIDEOUT KIDS

GRIZZLY BEARS
& BEAVER PELTS

MIKE GLEASON

HIDEOUT KIDS

MACHO NACHO
& THE COWBOY BATTLE

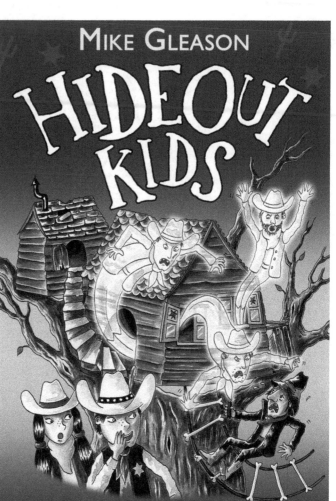

MIKE GLEASON

HIDEOUT KIDS

THE PARROT GANG
& WILD WEST CHOSTS

MR. ZIP

WILD THING

JUDGE JUNE

SPIKY

ABOUT THE AUTHOR

Hideout Kids author Mike Gleason comes from a small town in Texas. He grew up with cowboys, cowgirls and exciting stories of Wild West adventures. He was a wildcatter in the Texas oil fields and a board director at MGM in Hollywood. He created and produced an award-winning music television series at Abbey Road Studios. He lives and writes in London.

ABOUT THE ILLUSTRATOR

Hideout Kids illustrator Victoria Taylor comes from Cheltenham, England, and her love of art was inspired by her maternal grandmother. She trained at Plymouth University and worked for many years as a graphic designer. Having returned to her first love of painting and drawing, Victoria is now a freelance book illustrator. She lives in Gloucestershire with her husband and two children.

SANTA CLAUS.

A Visit From St. Nicholas: Twas the Night Before Christmas With Original 1849 Illustrations (Facsimile Edition)

by Clement C. Moore
Woodcuts by T.C. Boyd

This Edition, Hard Cover: ISBN — 978-1-947844-15-5
Also Available in Soft Cover:
ISBN — 978-1-947844-14-8

Discounts on bulk orders are available. Contact
publisher@suzeteo.com for more information.

Published by Suzeteo Enterprises,

SANTA CLAUS'S VISIT.

A

VISIT FROM
ST. NICHOLAS,

BY

CLEMENT C. MOORE, LL.D.

———

With Original Cuts,

DESIGNED AND ENGRAVED BY BOYD.

———

———

1849.

C

A

PRESENT

FOR

GOOD

LITTLE BOYS

AND

GIRLS.

VISIT FROM SANTA CLAUS.

'T WAS the night before Christmas,
    when all through the house
Not a creature was stirring, not
    even a mouse;
The stockings were hung by the
    chimney with care,
In hopes that St. Nicholas soon
    would be there;
The children were nestled all snug
    in their beds,
While visions of sugar-plums danced in their
    heads;
And Mamma in her 'kerchief, and I in my cap,
Had just settled our brains for a long winter's
    nap;

When out on the lawn there arose such a clatter,
I sprang from the bed to see what was the
   matter.
Away to the window I flew like a flash,
Tore open the shutters and threw up the sash.
The moon on the breast of the new-fallen snow,
Gave the lustre of mid-day to objects below,
When, what to my wondering eyes should
   appear,
But a miniature sleigh, and eight tiny rein-deer,
With a little old driver, so lively and quick,
I knew in a moment it must be St. Nick.
More rapid than eagles his coursers they came,
And he whistled, and shouted, and called them
   by name ;
" Now, *Dasher !* now, *Dancer !* now *Prancer*
   and *Vixen !*

On, *Comet !* on, *Cupid !* on, *Donder and Blitzen !*

To the top of the porch ! to the top of the wall !

Now dash away ! dash away ! dash away all !"

As dry leaves that before the wild hurricane fly,

When they meet with an obstacle, mount to the sky ;

So up to the house-top the coursers they flew,

With the sleigh full of Toys, and St. Nicholas too.

And then in a twinkling, I heard on the roof,

The prancing and pawing of each little hoof—

As I drew in my head, and was turning around,

Down the chimney St. Nicholas came with a
bound.

He was dressed all in fur, from his head to his
foot,

And his clothes were all tarnished with ashes
and soot ;

A bundle of Toys he had flung on his back,

And he looked like a pedlar just opening his
pack,

His eyes—how they twinkled ! his dimples
how merry !

His cheeks were like roses, his nose like a
cherry !

His droll little mouth was drawn up like a
bow,

And the beard of his chin was as white as the
snow ;

The stump of a pipe he held tight in his teeth,
And the smoke it encircled his head like a
    wreath ;
He had a broad face and a little round belly,
That shook when he laughed like a bowlfull
    of jelly.
He was chubby and plump, a right jolly old elf,
And I laughed when I saw him, in spite of
    myself,
A wink of his eye and a twist of his head,
Soon gave me to know I had nothing to dread ;
He spoke not a word, but went straight to his
    work,
And fill'd all the stockings ; then turned with
    a jerk,
And laying his finger aside of his nose,
And giving a nod, up the chimney he rose ;

He sprang to his sleigh, to his team gave a
    whistle,

And away they all flew like the down of a
    thistle.

But I heard him exclaim, ere he drove out of
    sight,

"HAPPY CHRISTMAS TO ALL, AND
TO ALL A GOOD NIGHT"

Printed in the USA
CPSIA information can be obtained
at www.ICGtesting.com
LVHW051454261023
761972LV00003B/77